Copyright © 2018 by Clavis Publishing Inc., New York

First published as *Ik en mijn auto's* in Belgium and Holland by Clavis Uitgeverij, Hasselt—Amsterdam, 2018
English translation from the Dutch by Clavis Publishing Inc., New York

Visit us on the Web at www.clavisbooks.com.

Me and My Cars written and illustrated by Liesbet Slegers

ISBN 978-1-60537-399-7

This book was printed in December 2017 at Wai Man Book Binding (China) Ltd. Flat A, 9/F.,
Phase 1, Kwun Tong Industrial Centre, 472-484 Kwun Tong Road, Kwun Tong, Kowloon, H.K.

First Edition
10 9 8 7 6 5 4 3 2 1

Clavis Publishing supports the First Amendment and celebrates the right to read

Liesbet Slegers

Me
and
My Cars

Clavis

NEW YORK

Want to come for a ride?

This is my **car**.
Daddy and I are going for a drive.
Buckle up!

This is a **bus**.
I look out the window.
Hello!

This is a **jeep**.
The jeep drives over rough and bumpy roads.
The big tires help.

This is a mobile **camper**.
It's a little house on wheels.
I sleep in my bed inside.

This is an **ice cream truck.**
The ice cream man sells cones and other treats.
I want one too. Yum!

This is a **moving van**.
It's big and long.
Lots of furniture fits inside.

This is a **delivery van**.
It has brought a package.
Maybe it's a surprise for me?

This is a **limousine**.
I see a girl with a crown!
I wave my flag. Hooray!

This is a **semi-truck**.
I'm at the wheel.
Beep beep!

This is a **tanker**.
The tanker carries milk
from the farm to the store.

This is a **car transporter**.
It carries new cars.
I count five cars.

Want to
help?

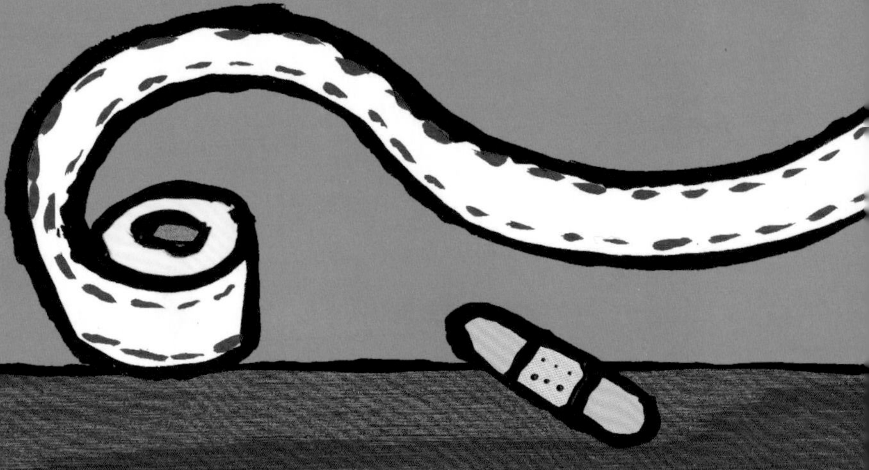

This is an **ambulance**.
The ambulance has a siren.
It carries people to the hospital.

This is a **police car.**
The police car drives to an accident.
The police are here to help.

This is a **police van**.
There are cones inside.
The police officer puts the cones on the road.

This is a **fire engine.**
The fire engine has a ladder and two hoses.
The firefighters put out the fire.

This is a **tow truck.**
The tow truck pulls a car
to the repair shop.
The car has a flat tire.

Want to get some work done?

This is a **tractor** with a **trailer**.
The trailer is full of hay.
"Cluck, cluck!" says the chicken.

This is a **garbage truck**.
The garbage collectors put
trash bags in the back.
Crunch! Now the trash is compacted.

This is a **street sweeper.**
It cleans the street with its brushes.
The street is clean again!

This is a **bulldozer**.
A bulldozer pushes dirt and stones away.
The bulldozer helps build a new road.

This is an **excavator**.
The excavator digs a hole.
Then it loads the dirt into a dump truck.

This is a **dump truck.**
The dump truck has a big trunk
filled with dirt.
The trunk goes up . . .
and the dirt pours out.

This is a **crane truck**.
The crane carries a heavy
piece of concrete.
The crane is very strong!

Want to
race along?

This is a **racecar**.
The racecar is very fast!
Watch it go!

These are **Formula 1 racecars.**
Which Formula 1 car do you
think will win the race?